ACADEMY OF DANCE

Hip-Hop
Road Trip

written by
Margaret Gurevich

illustrated by
Claire Almon

STONE ARCH BOOKS
a capstone imprint

Academy of Dance is published by Stone Arch Books,
A Capstone Imprint
1710 Roe Crest Drive
North Mankato, Minnesota 56003
www.mycapstone.com

Text and illustrations © 2019 Stone Arch Books

Library of Congress Cataloging-in-Publication Data
Names: Gurevich, Margaret, author. | Almon, Claire, illustrator.
Title: Hip-hop road trip / by Margaret Gurevich ; illustrated by Claire Almon.
Description: North Mankato, Minnesota : an imprint of Stone Arch Books,
[2018] | Series: Academy of Dance | Summary: Brie and the rest of the
dancers at Ms. Marianne's Academy of Dance are on their way to Florida
to compete in the Citrus Jam, which is held just outside of Orlando, and
where first place includes the opportunity to march in the Main Street parade
at Disney World—but the team from Austin, Texas, includes some girls
who are planning to sabotage the other competitors.
Identifiers: LCCN 2018005691| ISBN 9781496562043 (hardcover) |
ISBN 9781496562081 (pbk.)
Subjects: LCSH: Dance—Competitions—Juvenile fiction. | Dance teams—
Juvenile fiction. | Competition (Psychology)—Juvenile fiction. | Sabotage—
Juvenile fiction. | Walt Disney World (Fla.)—Juvenile fiction. | Florida—Juvenile
fiction. | CYAC: Dance teams—Fiction. | Competition (Psychology)—Fiction. |
Sabotage—Fiction. | Walt Disney World (Fla.)—Fiction. | Florida—Fiction.
Classification: LCC PZ7.G98146 Hi 2018 | DDC 813.6 [Fic]—dc23
LC record available at https://lccn.loc.gov/2018005691

Designer: Kay Fraser

Image Credits: To come

Printed and bound in Canada.
PA020

TABLE OF CONTENTS

CHAPTER 1

ROAD TRIP!

We've been on this bus for hours. The closer we get to Disneyworld, the more layers I peel off. No more gloves, hats, winter coats, or scarves. I'll take Florida heat over snowy New Jersey winters any day.

Gabby Sanchez, one of my best friends and a fellow dance-team member, yawns and stretches beside me. "Are we there yet?" she asks sleepily.

I shake my head. "No. But the Disney billboards must mean we're close."

"Can you believe it's really happening, Brie?" Gabby says, sounding more awake. "We'll get to perform in Disneyworld's Main Street parade!"

I laugh. "*If* we win."

Gabby rolls her eyes. "With your hip-hop skills," she says, voice rising, "my jazz team's killer routine, plus all of our ballet and tap combinations, there's no way we don't win. We're a quadruple threat!"

Behind me Jada Grant and Grace Jenkins, our two other best friends, whoop and playfully kick the back of the seats.

"You got that right!" sings Grace. She does a mini tap dance with her feet. Jada, meanwhile, strikes one of her many ballet poses.

I can't blame my friends for feeling confident. Ms. Marianne's Academy of Dance, where we all dance together, is a great school. If it wasn't, we wouldn't have made the cut for the Citrus Jam, a dance competition that takes place a few miles outside Orlando, Florida.

Dance instructors for teams in the twelve-and-over category had to submit audition tapes of their teams to qualify. Teams from all over the world applied, but only twenty were chosen to compete. It's a huge honor to be included.

"We should feel proud no matter what happens," I say. "First, second, and third place get trophies! Just the fact that we're here at all . . ." My voice trails off as my friends stare at me open-mouthed.

Grace groans. "A trophy is great, but imagine all of us dancing down Main Street!"

Ms. Marianne, our lead instructor, turns around in her seat. "I like that image too," she says. "But I want you all to keep something in mind: *every* team at this competition will be very talented."

"Not as talented as us!" shouts Gabby. Everyone cheers.

Ms. Marianne frowns. "That type of behavior," she says, "is what I *don't* want from you girls. Other teams might try to intimidate us. Unfortunately, that's not uncommon. But our team will be known not just for our skills but for our positive attitudes. If we win, it will be because we deserved it, not because we made someone else feel terrible."

"To awesome dancing," Grace cheers, pumping her first in the air.

Jada nudges her. "And to positive behavior!" she says, pumping her first in the air too.

Even Ms. Marianne laughs at that. "Atta girl!"

* * *

As we get off the bus, I drag my tired body into the hotel lobby to join my team. I can't wait to check in and fall into bed.

Suddenly I feel a hard poke between my shoulder blades. I spin around.

"Watch where you're going," a girl with braided blond hair snaps at me. She's wearing a sparkly T-shirt that says *AUSTIN ROCKS*.

My mouth goes dry, and I just stare. I'm confident onstage but am shy around new people. Rude new people make it even harder.

The braided girl turns to the girls beside her. They're all wearing *AUSTIN ROCKS* T-shirts. My heart sinks as I realize this is likely another dance team. Ms. Marianne's speech from the bus comes to mind.

"Hey," the braided girl says loudly, "do you have a problem?"

I don't know where Gabby, Grace, and Jada come from, but they're suddenly beside me.

"It sounds like *you're* the one with the problem," says Grace, eyes narrowed.

The girl and her friends laugh. Gabby steps forward so she's face-to-face with the girls, but they don't seem bothered.

The braided girl motions for her friends to follow her. "See you on Main Street, losers," she says. "We'll be the ones marching—"

"—while you're crying your eyes out!" a curly-haired girl finishes.

Gabby and Grace ball their hands into fists as the snarky girls leave the lobby.

"We'll see who's crying," Jada mumbles.

"What jerks!" says Grace.

Gabby puts her arm around me. "That's intimidation at its finest," she says with a small smile. "But we won't let them get to us, right?"

I'm still rooted to the same spot I was when all this started. I swallow. My stomach does somersaults.

"Right," I say shakily.

CHAPTER 2

FEARLESS BRIE

Back home at Ms. Marianne's, the practice studios are brightly lit. Sun streams through the large picture windows. The floors are smooth, glossy hardwood, and huge mirrors line the walls.

Our Orlando practice space isn't quite as picturesque. That's clear as soon as I arrive for practice the next morning. The hotel conference room we've been assigned has no windows or mirrors, and the hardwood floors are scratched up.

Shake it off, I tell myself. *Dancing can happen anywhere.*

Our instructor, Ms. Jackie, is waiting for me and the rest of the hip-hop team. She wastes no time, clapping her hands and motioning for us to get into position. I roll my head from side to side and get ready.

"We'll begin with the first five moves of our routine," says Ms. Jackie. "Tut, pivot, kickball change, kickball down, knee spin." She lists them off on her fingers.

Everyone nods. We begin with our heads down and arms crossed. When the music starts, we walk forward. Tutting is quick movements and sharp angles, like robot moves but faster.

I bring my palms together and bend my elbows, like a genie, then quickly sink down to a *plié*. My knees rotate inward so they touch, then turn back out into a *plié*. In unison, we all spring back up and thrust our fists in the air, circling them round, as we complete our pivot turns.

"Add some funk!" Ms. Jackie calls as we bend low for the kickball change.

Bam! I kick my right foot out to the side before stepping out with my left.

"And down!" Ms. Jackie calls. We all kick out again, then get down on one knee. "Now spin!"

I stay on my left knee and use my arms to help me spin around.

"Well done, girls!" Ms. Jackie says. She stops the music and opens the door to let more air in. "You ready for more?"

"Yes!" my teammates and I all shout.

For once I'm just as loud as everyone else. I'm normally shy, but when that music comes on, I become tough, cool, and confident. I'm fearless, not the tongue-tied girl the Austin team met yesterday.

"OK!" Ms. Jackie calls. "Let's pick it up with the baby freeze."

I crouch low, bending my right leg and putting my left knee on the ground. I cross my left elbow over my right knee, then move my right arm to the side of my body, back toward my hip.

Now comes the hard part: balance. I place both palms on the floor and lift my body off the ground, resting my right knee on my elbows and my head on the floor.

"Keep the knees in the air," Ms. Jackie says, "and cross them back and forth."

I sway but manage to keep my legs up.

"Keep at it, ladies!"

I need a water break, but Ms. Jackie's enthusiasm motivates me to keep going. *Rock step, glide, and pin drop.* I jump up, kick my right leg out, and cross it over my left. *Rock back on the left heel and step on the right. Rock and step*, I think as I repeat the move on my left leg.

"Glide!" Ms. Jackie calls.

I bend my right knee and lift my heel off the ground. Then I push off and move my left foot to the side so it looks like it's gliding across the floor.

"Excellent!" Ms. Jackie says. "Pin drop!"

I repeat the glide with my left foot and fall to the floor, legs crossed. The pin drop reminds me of those gym exercises where we rise from sitting cross-legged without using our hands.

Spin around and up, I think.

Ms. Jackie turns off the music and claps loudly. "Fifteen-minute water break, then we'll take it from the top! Tomorrow we'll perfect the end of the routine."

I wipe my face and neck with a towel, take a large swig from my water bottle, and head to the hallway. I need to get some air after that run-through.

I set my water bottle on the floor beside me as I lean back against the wall. Closing my eyes, I picture the moves we just did.

"That was brilliant!"

My eyes pop open. A girl dressed in a black tank top, baggy black pants, and sneakers is smiling at me.

"Me?" I ask.

"Definitely. Those were some *serious* moves." She adjusts her rhinestone-studded hat. "I'm Olivia, by the way," she says with an accent.

"Thanks," I say, clutching my towel. "Um, I'm Brie."

Olivia extends one hand to me and motions at something with her other. That's when I notice a few other girls standing around the lobby.

"Those are my mates," she says as the girls walk over.

For a moment, I panic. Meeting new people is hard enough. Being sweaty and gross while doing it is even worse. I force myself to channel Fearless Brie.

"Where are you from?" asks Olivia.

"New Jersey. You?"

"London," one of Olivia's friends replies. She's wearing a purple tank and matching baseball cap. "It was fierce cold there!"

I'm guessing *fierce* means *very* in this context. "Super cold in Jersey too."

"Where are your mates?" the girl asks.

I like London speak. "Probably in one of the other conference rooms."

Just then we hear squeals and laughter from outside the lobby. "Austin in the house!" someone shouts.

My stomach clenches. That's all it takes for Fearless Brie to disappear.

CHAPTER 3

Austin Baddies

The Austin team, dressed in shorts and cute sleeveless tops, is clearly done with practice. The girl who poked me yesterday cartwheels toward us. Another does the splits behind her. Gabby's words—*intimidation at its finest*—echo in my head.

"Hey," says Olivia. She introduces herself and her friends to the newcomers, but I'm so distracted, I only catch one name—Emily, the girl in the purple cap.

"I'm Liz," the girl who did the cartwheel replies. She cracks her gum.

"Kelsey," the splits girl adds. "We're from Texas." She blows a bubble.

"*Austin*, Texas," Liz stresses. "There's a team from Dallas staying in the hotel down the road. They've got *nothing* on us."

Kelsey nods and cracks her gum. "Where are ya'll from?"

"London," says Olivia. She doesn't seem the least bit intimidated.

Liz squints at me. "Didn't we meet you yesterday?"

I nod.

Kelsey and Liz laugh. "Looks like she still doesn't know how to talk," Liz taunts.

"Can you tell us where you're from?" Kelsey asks. She says it slowly, like she's talking to a toddler.

Tears push at the back of my eyes. I try to stand tall, despite wanting to disappear. "New Jersey."

Liz smirks. "Figures."

What's that supposed to mean? I think. But I don't say anything.

Emily, however, doesn't stay quiet. She narrows her eyes. "Why's that? Did you hear all the best dancers are from New Jersey?"

Liz snorts. "Yeah, that must be it." She waves at her friends to follow her as she starts walking away. "Don't practice too hard!"

Just then one of her teammates hands her something. Liz cackles and turns back to me. "Catch," she says, tossing something in my direction.

I catch it instinctively. *My water bottle!* I realize.

Liz stops to watch my reaction. The water has bits of dirt floating in it . . . and there's something else. Shoelaces! Gross!

"Enjoy your drink!" Liz laughs as she and her friends leave the lobby.

Olivia scowls. "I can't believe they did that! Girls like that make me so mad! You should tell someone."

Before I can reply, Ms. Jackie sticks her head out the door. "Time to get back in!" she calls.

"Nice meeting you," I say, walking back to the conference room. I'm angry, not just at the Austin girls but at myself too. Where did Fierce Brie go? Why didn't I stick up for my team?

I try to fight off the sick feeling in my stomach. I think about what Ms. Marianne said about positive behavior and intimidation.

Ignore them, I tell myself. *Don't stoop to their level.*

I want Liz and Kelsey to know what New Jersey dancers are made of. I just hope I can get up the nerve to show them.

CHAPTER 4

PLAYING DIRTY

Grace, Gabby, Jada, and I spend the next morning at Disney. We're on our way to Space Mountain when Grace stops to witness the Main Street parade.

"Look, you guys," she exclaims. She stands on her tiptoes to see over the sea of people in front of us. Mickey and Elsa wave from their floats as a high school band marches behind them.

"That could be us next week," Jada whispers, clutching Grace's arm.

"That *will* be us," Gabby says.

"*Will* be us," someone mimics.

The four of us turn around. Kelsey and Liz are standing behind us.

When did they get here? I wonder.

"*Excuse* me?" says Gabby, her eyes flashing mad.

It's already a tight space, but Liz and Kelsey squeeze in closer. "I just wouldn't be so confident if I were you."

"Leave us alone," I mumble.

"How was your sewer water?" Kelsey asks, smirking at me.

Grace sucks in air through her teeth. I told them last night about what happened at practice. "Dancing well isn't enough?" she says. "You want to get the other teams sick too?"

Liz's face turns red as she glares at us. "Maybe we just care more about winning than you do," she says.

"Right," says Kelsey, "anything goes."

The hair on my arms stands on end, but I try to sound brave. "We're out of here," I say. My voice catches.

"I'd run scared too!" Liz calls after us as we walk away.

No one bothers to respond. We walk out of the huddle, not turning around until we're far enough away that they won't see us.

"I know Ms. Marianne said we should be known for our dancing and positive behavior, but this is ridiculous!" Gabby finally says.

Grace shrugs. "They're just trying to psych us out."

"It's more than that," says Jada. "What if Brie accidentally drank that garbage yesterday?"

I nervously wring my hands. "If they strike again, I'll figure out what to do. It's just . . ." My voice trails off.

Jada squeezes my shoulder. "Hard," she finishes for me. "We know."

I'm grateful my friends get me. We get in line to buy humongous turkey legs, and I try to put our run-in out of my mind.

"Brie!" I hear from the back of the line. It's Olivia and Emily. I wave, and they hurry over.

I quickly introduce them. "Guys, this is Emily and Olivia. I met them on break yesterday too. They're on the London team."

When we've all gotten our turkey legs, the four of us fill the other girls in on our most recent confrontation with the Austin troublemakers.

"What jerks!" says Emily.

Olivia takes a sip of her soda. "They're playing dirty, and I don't like it."

I bite my lip. "Maybe they'll feel like they've done enough to intimidate us and stop now," I say hopefully.

Gabby shakes her head. "I don't think so."

A pit grows in my stomach. Something needs to be done about Austin. Standing up for myself is a start, but even *thinking* about that makes me nervous.

A hand waves in front of my face. "Come back, Brie!" jokes Jada.

I force a smile.

"We'll figure everything out together," says Gabby, giving me a hug.

"We'll help," say Olivia and Emily.

Grace licks her fingers and throws out the rest of her turkey leg. "Space Mountain will make us brave!" she says.

I laugh as the six of us walk to the long line stretching before us. Brave Brie, Fierce Brie, Tough Brie. If only the answer were as simple as changing my name.

CHAPTER 5

FEEL THE ENERGY

"Let's work on the last section of our routine," Ms. Jackie says at practice the next day. "Then we'll take it from the top."

Like a scarecrow, I bend my elbows and knees inward for the lock move. Then I straighten my legs and raise my elbows up to do the lock again. This time my arms look like I'm flexing.

Strong, Fierce, I think. Hip-hop Brie is a totally different girl than the one Austin pushes around.

"Good locking, girls! Knee spin, split!" Ms. Jackie shouts to be heard above the music.

I get down on the ground and spin on my knee, then spread my legs for the splits. My palms land behind me on the floor, close to my lower back, for the shootout. My knees touch and move toward my chest. Like lightning, my heels shoot out in front of me, legs straight. I lean my head back, then quickly bring my knees to my chest again.

"Body roll," Ms. Jackie tells us. "Then pop it!"

I rise from the floor and roll my body up like a snake trying to reach the ceiling. Then I bend my knees and raise my right arm to the side, wrist down.

"Remember the string," says Ms. Jackie.

When we first learned this move, Ms. Jackie told us to pretend we were marionettes, and strings were pulling at our hands and arms. I picture the string now, pulling my elbow up to my shoulder, while my wrist straightens.

"Feel the energy pulsing through your arm, all the way to your fingertips," Ms. Jackie calls.

I feel it. I move my wrist back down and feel the electricity moving back up my arm to my shoulder until it pops back up. I peek at the other dancers as the energy rises from my toes. It's as if I can hear the *pop pop pop* of each move.

"Wrap it up!" Ms. Jackie calls. "Side shuffle and clap."

I move my left foot to the side and follow with my right. *Clap.* Right to the side and follow with my left. *Clap.*

Everyone gets in line for the final move. One at a time, like falling dominos, we all sink to identical *pliés* and rest our elbows on our knees.

Ms. Jackie turns off the music and applauds. "Great work, girls! I have a good feeling about Sunday."

That's it, I tell myself. *Stay focused on dance, forget about Austin, and you'll feel the same.*

* * *

That night Gabby's snoring keeps me awake. Finally I can't take it anymore. I get dressed and head to the lobby. As I walk in, I see Liz and Kelsey huddled in the corner.

I pause, not sure what to do. Then I inch closer but stay in the shadows.

"I'm not doing it," Kelsey hisses.

"Then you're not serious," Liz snaps. "*Some* of us have worked too hard to lose."

Kelsey's nostrils flare. "I have worked hard! I want to win too."

"Prove it," Liz says, putting her hands on her hips. "Stick to the plan." She takes her room key out of her pocket, holds it between her fingers, and waves it in front of Kelsey's face.

Kelsey steps back, but Liz keeps waving. "Prove it," she says again.

"You're being ridiculous," Kelsey says shakily.

Liz shrugs and sticks her key back in her pocket. "Whatever, coward. My *real* teammates will help me. And then the other teams will be out of the running."

Liz starts to walk away, but Kelsey grabs her arm. "Don't," she pleads. "If you're caught—"

Liz snatches her arm away. "I'm not a dummy," she growls.

"Clearly," says Kelsey, wiping a tear with the back of her hand, "you are."

"Whatever," Liz sneers. "When we win, remember to thank me."

Kelsey chokes back a sob and runs down the hall. Liz walks in the opposite direction.

Liz is up to something. That much is obvious. But what? I rush back to my room.

"Gabs!" I say, jumping on her bed.

She moans and turns to her other side.

"Gabby!" I say louder, nudging her arm.

She turns toward the clock on our nightstand. "Brie, it's three in the morning. What gives?"

"This is important!" I bounce on the bed and turn on the lights.

Gabby glares at me. "Is this about your hip-hop routine? You're awesome. Go to sleep." She turns away from me, but I turn on all the lights.

"Brie!" she growls.

"I just overheard Liz and Kelsey in the lobby. I think Liz is up to something. I'm worried she's going to sabotage the other teams," I say breathlessly.

Gabby bolts upright, fully awake now. "What? No way! How do you know?"

I quickly tell her what I saw and heard.

"We have to tell someone," says Gabby.

"I thought about that," I reply, tapping my lips with my finger. "But we need evidence. Otherwise she'll just deny it."

Gabby nods in agreement. "It's too late to do anything now. Let's talk to Jada and Grace tomorrow."

"And Olivia and Emily," I add. "Maybe we can figure this out together."

"Let's get some sleep in the meantime," says Gabby hopefully. She hits the lights and lays back down. Two minutes later, I hear snoring.

How can she do that? I wonder.

I lie down and fluff up my pillow. Finally, I fall asleep too. I'm not sure what I dream about, but I spend most of the night tossing and turning. When I wake five hours later, I don't feel rested at all.

CHAPTER 6

Whatever It Takes

The next morning, we gather the other girls in the lobby and brainstorm.

"Wait," says Olivia, "tell us what you heard again."

I repeat it, making sure to leave nothing out. "What could the plan be?" I ask.

"I don't know. But if we figure it out," says Emily, "we'll know what to do."

Olivia gasps. "Shhh!" She turns her head toward the other side of the lobby.

We all stare as Liz, Kelsey, and a curly-haired girl in a pink leotard and jazz shoes enter. The three of them are deep in conversation.

"Who's *she*?" asks Grace.

"That's the girl we met in the lobby our first day," I say, recognizing her. "The one who told us we'd be crying our eyes out while they're marching on Main Street."

"That can't be good," says Jada.

Liz glares at Kelsey, and the curly-haired girl stomps her foot. Finally she and Liz storm off, leaving Kelsey alone on the couch.

"Looks like another fight," says Gabby.

The nervous feeling in my stomach comes back. "I wish I knew what they were up to," I say.

"Same," mumbles Gabby.

"Based on what Liz said," I say, "she'll do whatever it takes to win."

Olivia sighs. "We'll just have to keep an eye out. Nothing we can do about it without proof."

"I guess," says Emily. "But I hate letting things go."

Grace looks at her phone. "Practice starts in ten minutes."

"How are we supposed to focus?" asks Jada.

I narrow my eyes and spring off the couch, ready to dance. Austin may give me butterflies, but dancing is one thing I can handle. "We'll just have to."

* * *

On Saturday morning, Gabby and I find a note under our door: *All-team meeting in the lobby @ 10 AM.*

"What's this about?" I ask.

"Only one way to find out," Gabby replies. She jumps up and gets dressed in minutes.

I do the same. "I've never seen you move this fast in the morning," I tease.

Gabby laughs. "I'm full of surprises," she says as we head out of our room.

We run into Grace and Jada in the hallway. Emily and Olivia are with them.

"You all have a meeting too?" I ask.

"Weird, right?" says Emily.

"I thought they meant just *our* team," I say. We all stop walking, obviously thinking the same thing.

"Do the judges know something?" Emily asks.

"We'll know soon enough," I say as we walk into the lobby. The disappointed faces of our instructors are waiting for us.

CHAPTER 7

Moment of Truth

A small, frizzy-haired woman walks to the center of the lobby. "I'm Ms. Price, the head of the Citrus Jam," she introduces herself. "I'm sorry to have to tell you this, but last night the room holding everyone's costumes was broken into. Some costumes were damaged."

The room erupts in questions and gasps.

"Damaged how?" asks Emily.

"Cut, painted . . . it's a mess," says Ms. Price.

All the dancers' eyes fill with angry tears. I search for the Austin team and find them on the couch farthest from everyone else. Kelsey wipes away tears. Her teammates look stunned.

Then I see Liz and the curly-haired girl from the other day. They don't look sad at all.

"Ladies," says Ms. Price, "you've all worked too hard for things to end like this. If anyone has any information, please see me or your dance instructors." She walks to the front desk.

Suddenly it hits me. "You guys," I whisper, "it wasn't her key."

"Huh?" asks Emily confused.

"What Liz was holding," I say quickly. "I assumed it was her room key, but what if it wasn't? What if it was the key to the costume room? Think about it. If she had a key, it would be easy to sneak into the room, vandalize the costumes, and get out."

"That's true . . .," Olivia says slowly. "Ms. Price said *some* costumes were damaged, not *all*. I mean, she wouldn't damage her own team's costumes."

We sit quietly and think about what could have happened. Liz and the curly-haired girl are smirking and not trying to hide it.

I get up from the couch. I'm almost at the front desk before I realize what I'm about to do. Shy, non-confrontational Brie is going to say what she saw.

You can do it. I take a deep breath.

"Ms. Jackie," I say quietly. "I think I know what happened . . ."

* * *

At dinner that night, the disqualified Austin team is all anyone can talk about.

When Ms. Price confronted Liz, she confessed. She stole the key from her instructor, and she and a few of her teammates paid attention to the cleaning crew's schedule. Then they snuck in and sabotaged some of the costumes.

Fortunately the Citrus Jam employs a talented team of costume designers. They'll be able to fix some of the damage.

Also fortunate, Liz and her friends didn't really think their plan through. When the crew came back earlier than expected, they had to split. That's why only some of the costumes had been tampered with.

"You're a hero!" shouts Grace.

"Please," I say, blushing.

Ever since word got out that I helped find the culprits, dancers from other states and countries have been coming up to hug and thank me. I don't think I've ever blushed so much in my life.

"If this isn't a good sign for tomorrow," says Gabby, "I don't know what is!"

CHAPTER 8

AND THE WINNER IS . . .

"Break a leg," Grace whispers backstage the next day.

I close my eyes and picture myself dancing my hardest.

"New Jersey!" I hear the announcer call through the curtain, and we take our places onstage.

The curtain rises, lights illuminate the stage, and music comes on. We strut forward and begin the tutting. I clasp my palms, and my knees snap together and apart.

Pivot, I think as we all thrust our fists into the air and turn. I add some attitude into my kickball change and sway my hips a bit as my feet kick out.

The sparkles on our pants glitter under the lights as we spin on our knees. Our moves are crisp and fast as we place our palms on the floor for the baby freeze.

Balance! Ms. Jackie's voice rings in my ears as I cross my knees back and forth in the air. There's no swaying today.

Grrriiinder, I think. My right leg swings toward my left ankle, and I jump over it at the same time.

I feel pumped. *Rock and step*, I tell myself as I take turns rocking on my left and right heels. My left heel comes off the ground for the glide. *Whoosh.* I feel so light, like I'm actually sliding across the floor.

Just a few more moves. I'm back on the floor, sitting cross-legged. Just as quickly, I'm up again.

Lock. My elbows and knees turn inward, and we're all scarecrows. Then *phwoosh!* Back on the floor for the knee spins and splits.

Shootout time! My knees spring back together and toward my chest. My heels come out in front of me as if they're attached to a bungee cord.

Pop it! A buzz runs through me as the energy runs up my wrist to my shoulder.

The whole team sizzles as we step to the side and clap. We rest our elbows on our knees down, down, down the line.

My heart pounds, and my breath comes in short gasps. We link hands and take a bow as the curtain falls. Now we wait.

* * *

An hour later, we're sitting in the back of the auditorium, waiting for the results.

"This is the worst part," says Gabby.

"It is," I say, sipping my water, "but it isn't. The waiting is hard, but at least I don't have to worry if I'll miss my cue or something."

Gabby smiles. "I get that."

Finally the red light on the judges' table goes on, meaning they're ready. They hand the results to Ms. Price, who makes her way onstage.

"First off I want to thank all our dancers for participating. You were all wonderful," she begins. "Our three top teams will all receive trophies. First place, as you all know, will also march in tomorrow's Main Street parade at Disney."

"Just get on with it," Gabby mutters.

I giggle and give her a gentle shove.

"Third place," says Ms. Price, "goes to the team from Dallas, Texas."

The crowd applauds, and Gabby shifts impatiently in her seat.

"Second place is awarded to our dancers from London, England."

Cheers erupt from the back as Olivia and Emily's team rushes the stage.

"And finally, first place," says Ms. Price.

Beside me, Grace and Jada inhale sharply. Gabby squirms.

Come on, come on, come on, I think. *Please be us.*

"First place goes to . . ." Ms. Price pauses. "Ms. Marianne's Academy of Dance from New Jersey!"

We scream. Suddenly I'm onstage but don't remember walking there. Lights flash as our pictures are taken.

I stand frozen. *Is this real? Is it really happening?* Gabby squeezes one of my hands and Jada the other. I'm brought back to reality. It *is* real, and I take it all in.

CHAPTER 9

MY BEST SELF

Later that evening, I lean back on the soft lobby couches, stretch my legs, close my eyes, and wait for the rest of my team so we can have a celebratory dinner. The events from hours earlier are still fresh in my mind. The flashes from the cameras, the trophy, the applause.

Clap, clap, clap.

For a second, I think the applause is in my head, but it gets louder. My eyes snap open. Liz is standing in front of me.

"You must be super proud of yourself," she says sarcastically.

As usual, my mouth goes dry and my stomach seizes. Then I force myself to take a deep breath. *You got this, Brie.* I raise my head so our eyes meet.

"I actually am," I say.

Liz rolls her eyes. "I guess you were too scared to see what would have happened if we stayed in the competition."

Her words sound so crazy, I can't help laughing. "*I* was scared? You ruined all these costumes because *you* were afraid of the other teams' skills."

Liz's face twitches. I can see my words got to her. Giggling and chatter echo down the hallways. Suddenly Jada, Grace, and Gabby are by my side.

"What's going on?" asks Jada, arms crossed.

"I saw your team waiting for the elevators," says Gabby. "Why aren't you with them?"

Liz ignores them and tries to stare me down.

"Just so you know," she says in a fake sweet voice, "the Main Street parade is no joke. Hope you can handle it."

"Hey!" Grace yells, but I put my hand up to let her know I'm fine.

"I can," I say confidently. "But thanks for the concern."

Liz's jaw tenses. She seems irritated that her intimidation tactics aren't working on me anymore.

"Liz!" calls her dance teacher. "We're leaving."

Liz looks at the four of us one last time. Her eyes linger on me, but she doesn't say anything. Finally she walks away.

"Wow," says Gabby, "check you out."

"You weren't afraid of her at all!" says Grace.

"I wasn't," I say in disbelief.

"I guess you don't need us anymore," Jada jokes.

I roll my eyes. "Of course I need you! But maybe the next time someone tries to intimidate us, *I'll* be the one coming to the rescue!"

CHAPTER 10

MARCH IT OUT

Jada, Grace, Gabby, and I link arms and tilt our heads toward the warm Florida sun.

A float with Mickey, Donald, Elsa, and Anna stands in front of us. Acrobatic dancers adjust their sparkly leotards. The rhinestones on our own costumes shimmer in the sunlight.

"I can't believe we're here," I whisper.

"My stomach is flipping all over the place," says Grace.

"Same here," says Jada.

I bring my heel behind me for a stretch. "I feel like I'm going to jump out of my skin, but in a good way."

"Me too!" Gabby exclaims. "Didn't I call this, though?"

"Hey," say Olivia and Emily, walking over to us.

I give them a hug. "I wasn't sure if you guys were coming."

"We just came by to wish you luck," Olivia says. "Our flight leaves this afternoon, and we wanted to explore a little."

"So you're not staying?" I ask, disappointed.

"I'm sorry," says Olivia. "Why don't you all enter your emails into my phone?"

"Great idea!" I beam.

We type in our emails, and they promise to write. As I watch them walk away, I realize that as cool as a trophy is, I'm so grateful to be standing here right now.

The parade director walks over. "We're starting in five minutes," he says.

"We'd better get with our groups," I say, walking to my hip-hop team as Jada, Gabby, and Grace walk to their ballet, jazz, and tap teams.

There's an excited buzz of voices around us. Jasmine, Moana, Olaf, and other Disney characters get onto their floats. The band and majorettes pick up their instruments and batons. Drums beat, and music swells.

This is it, I think as the band begins marching. Our ballerinas pirouette across the cobblestones, and jazz dancers leap in the air. Grace's tap group shuffles and steps, creating fun *click-clack* sounds with their feet. Then it's hip-hop time.

I bring my hands together, praying style, creating sharp angles with my elbows. *In and out*, I think as I bring my knees together and apart.

I get close to the ground and swing my right leg toward my left for the coffee grinders, then become a wiggling inch worm as I shimmy up for the body roll.

The crowd applauds, and I grin. I think about how things could have turned out very differently if I hadn't found the courage to speak up about Liz's plot.

There's so much this trip has taught me. I can't pack Florida weather, but I can bring home the new me. The me who's confident and fierce—and not just onstage.

ABOUT THE AUTHOR

Margaret Gurevich is the author of many books for kids, including Capstone's *Gina's Balance, Aerials and Envy*, and the award-winning Chloe by Design series. She has also written for *National Geographic Kids* and Penguin Young Readers. While Margaret hasn't done performance dance since she was a tween, this series has inspired her to take dance classes again. She lives in New Jersey with her son and husband.

ABOUT THE ILLUSTRATOR

Claire Almon lives and works in Atlanta, Georgia, and holds a BFA in illustration from Ringling College of Art and Design, as well as an MFA in animation from Savannah College of Art and Design. She has worked for clients such as American Greetings, Netflix, and Cartoon Network and has taught character design at Savannah College of Art and Design. She specializes in creating fun, dynamic characters and works in a variety of mediums, including watercolor, pen and ink, pastel, and digital.

GLOSSARY

culprit (KUHL-prit)—someone who is guilty of
doing something wrong or of committing a crime

evidence (EV-uh-duhnss)—a collection of information
or facts that prove if something is true or not

fortunate (FOR-chuhn-it)—having good luck

intimidate (in-TIM-uh-date)—to threaten in order
to force certain behavior

marionette (mar-ee-uh-NET)—a puppet, usually
made of wood, that you move by pulling strings or
wires attached to parts of its body

plot (PLOT)—a secret plan, usually to do something
wrong or illegal

sabotage (SAB-uh-tahzh)—to damage, destroy,
or interfere with on purpose

tactic (TACK-tick)—an action planned to get
specific results

vandalize (VAN-duhl-ize)—to needlessly damage
property

TALK ABOUT IT!

1. Competitions can be fun, but they can also be challenging. Discuss some of the benefits and problems that come from doing something you love—like dancing— competitively.

2. Do you think Brie and her friends were right not to tell an adult when they sensed the Austin team was planning something? How would you have handled the situation?

3. Bullying can be more than just mean—it can be dangerous. Talk about some ways to combat bullying if you see it happening.

WRITE ABOUT IT!

1. Brie feels she has two sides: the fierce, fearless girl she is when she's dancing and the shy girl she is offstage. Write about the different parts of your personality. What brings the different parts out?

2. Brie and her friends decide, together, how to deal with the Austin team. Write about a time you relied on your friends to make a hard decision or to handle something difficult.

3. Dancing in the Main Street parade is a big deal for Brie and her fellow dancers. What's something you've done that felt similarly important? How did you deal with the pressure and the outcome, good or bad?

HIP-HOP TERMINOLOGY

There are two distinct styles of hip-hop dance: new school and old school. Old school focuses on original forms of hip-hop music or dance (breaking, popping, and locking) that evolved in the 1970s and 1980s. New school focuses on newer forms of hip-hop music or dance (house, krumping, voguing, street jazz) that emerged in the 1990s.

Want to learn more about hip-hop dance? Read on to learn some of the signature terms and moves:

battle—an event in which hip-hop dancers compete, usually in an open circle surrounded by other fans and competitors

B-boying—this eclectic style arrived on the early hip-hop scene in the 1970s and drew inspiration from a large number of musical, dance, and martial arts traditions. "Break boys and girls" soon became competitive and well-known for their style. The term *breakdancing* comes from this tradition.

beatboxing—using one's mouth to create rhythmic patterns and percussion sounds

freestyling—dancing (or rapping) without choreography (or lyrics); an improvised dance

isolation—a movement that involves singling out a body part and moving it while keeping the rest of your body still

locking—a playful staccato style developed on the West Coast; dancers move quickly through a series of split-second moves

plié—a French dance term borrowed from ballet; many hip-hop moves are performed in *plié* with knees bent

popping—variant of locking in which poses are linked into more fluid movement

robot—an early form of popping made famous by Michael Jackson

THE FUN DOESN'T STOP HERE!

DISCOVER MORE AT
WWW.CAPSTONEKIDS.COM